RIDERS

WHALE SONG OF PUFFIN CLIFF

WRITTEN BY JEN MAYLIN

ILLUSTRATED BY M

HARPER

An Imprint of HarperCollins

D1469085

With special thanks to Erin Falligant

Wind Riders #4: Whale Song of Puffin Cliff
Text copyright © 2022 by Working Partners Ltd.
Illustrations copyright © 2022 by HarperCollins Publishers
All rights reserved. Printed in the United States of America.
No part of this book may be used or reproduced in any manner whatsoever without written permission except in the case of brief quotations embodied in critical articles and reviews. For information address HarperCollins Children's Books, a division of HarperCollins Publishers, 195 Broadway, New York, NY 10007.
www.harpercollinschildrens.com

Library of Congress Control Number: 2022934065
ISBN 978-0-06-302939-2 (paperback) — ISBN 978-0-06-302940-8 (hardcover)

Typography by Joe Merkel
22 23 24 25 26 PC/LSCC 10 9 8 7 6 5 4 3 2 1
❖
First Edition

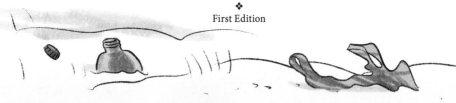

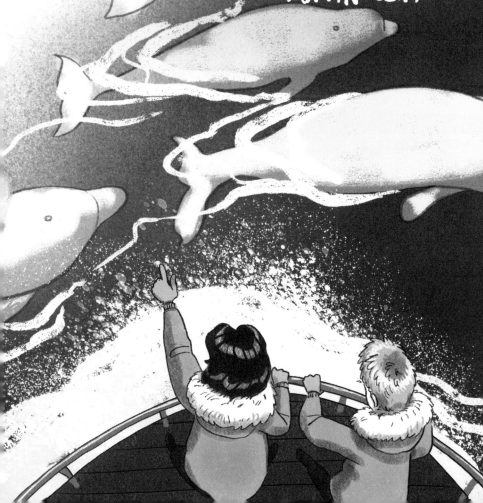

For Stacey and her beloved Whaley

CONTENTS

CHAPTER 1
SAND CRABS AND SEA GLASS

Sofia swam through the surf, keeping her snorkel above the shallow waves. Reaching down to the seabed, she scooped up stones and shells with her bucket. Then she popped her head out of the water, searching for Max. Her sandy-haired

friend was already on the beach, his snorkeling gear resting beside him.

"Come see what I found!" Max called to her.

Sofia raced out of the waves so fast, she nearly tripped over her flippers.

Max held two clear, sparkling stones in front of his eyes. "One blue eye, one green," he said. "Aren't they beautiful?" He batted his eyelashes.

Sofia swatted his shoulder playfully. "That's sea glass! Hey, I wonder if I found any." She dumped out her bucket, searching for colorful bits of glass worn smooth by the churning sea.

"A sand dollar," said Max, pointing. "You're rich!"

Sofia held up the round white object with the star etched across its top. "I'd take this over a real dollar any day," she said, imagining the tiny sea animal it had once been. She reached for a gray shell in the pile, then froze. The gray shell was *moving*.

Max scooped it up. "A sand crab! Hey, little guy." The crab's legs tickled his palm. When he set it down, it wiggled its V-shaped antennae and burrowed into the sand.

"Cute!" said Sofia, pushing her hair out of her eyes. "I've read about sand crabs."

"Me too— Well, Grandpa taught me about them." Max lived in Starry Bay with Grandpa, a retired fisherman. He shaded his eyes and searched the marina for their fishing boat, which bobbed gently on the sparkling waves. He had spent almost as much time on that boat as on dry land,

and Grandpa had taught him everything he knew about sea creatures.

Sofia knew tons about all kinds of animals, though. Her mom was a vet, and she was visiting Starry Bay for the summer with her parents.

Just then Max spotted a bit of orange plastic sticking out of Sofia's shell pile. He reached for the scrap of plastic and groaned. A blue cartoon fish grinned at him from the Bay Fish Grill logo.

"Trash," said Sofia, wrinkling her fore-head.

Max nodded. "Plastic from a fast-food restaurant. There's way too much of it in the ocean."

Sofia jumped to her feet. "Let's recycle it!" She grabbed the plastic and waddled toward the nearest recycling bin, not even pausing to take off her flippers.

When she got back, Max pointed out a frosted white triangle in her shell pile. "You *did* find some sea glass."

"It looks like ice!" said Sofia. But as she

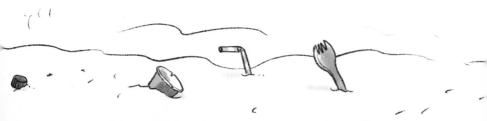

held up the glass, a seagull  swooped down and snatched it from her fingertips. "Hey!" she cried.

Instead of flying away with its prize, the gull landed nearby and dropped the sea glass in the sand. Then it swiveled its white head, staring at them with dark, mysterious eyes.

"It's *our* seagull," Max whispered, excitement tingling down his spine. The gull showed up when it was time for another adventure on *Wind Rider*, a magical sailboat that they had found hidden in the mangrove forest beside the beach.

Sofia leaped up. "Let's get to the boat!" she cried.

"Wait," said Max, laughing. "Don't you want to take off your duck feet?"

Sofia glanced down. "Oh. Ha!" She kicked off her flippers and quickly got dressed. Then she sprinted after the gull, along the beach toward the boardwalk that led to the mangrove forest.

As she stepped into the cool, damp forest, shadows crisscrossed her path. She pushed through tangled leaves and branches until she reached the clearing where she knew *Wind Rider* lay waiting.

The old sailboat rested like a beached whale, half in the water and half out. Its weathered boards had faded to gray, and its tattered sail waved gently, as if greeting Sofia.

When Max caught up to her, he sighed happily. *Wind Rider* looked like a wrecked old boat, but Max knew better. He and Sofia had sailed to faraway places on this magical boat. *Wind Rider* always returned them right here to the mangrove forest, with no time having passed—as if they'd never been gone at all. But, oh, the adventures they'd had!

"*Caw!*" the seagull cried from the broken deck rail.

Max laughed. "All right already," he said. "We're coming!"

Sofia scampered up the ladder and onto the deck ahead of him. She followed the gull until it landed on the helm—an old wooden steering wheel.

The moment Max joined Sofia and placed his hand on the helm, the wind picked up. Leaves swirled and branches creaked. Overhead, the tattered sails of *Wind Rider* began to unfurl. "I wonder where we're going," said Max.

"Do you think there'll be animals that need our help?" asked Sofia, her stomach fluttering. *Wind Rider* always brought them just where they were needed most.

"*Caw!*" The seagull hopped off the helm as it began to move, and both kids let go. As the wooden wheel creaked in a slow circle, Max grinned. "You won't have to wait long to find out. Hold on!"

CHAPTER 2
THE WHiSTLiNG WHALE

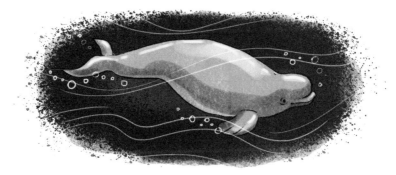

As the helm whirled around, *Wind Rider* began to rock. Max covered his eyes against the raging wind with one hand. Through his fingers, he saw green leaves swirl past. Then blue sky. Then charcoal-colored rocks—no, *mountains*. The wind was much colder than it had been a moment ago.

Beside him, Sofia laughed out loud. *It's like a ride at the fair!* she thought, squatting to keep her balance. But when the wind slowed, she popped up like a jack-in-the-box.

She admired the sailboat's polished deck and crisp white sails. *Wind Rider* looked

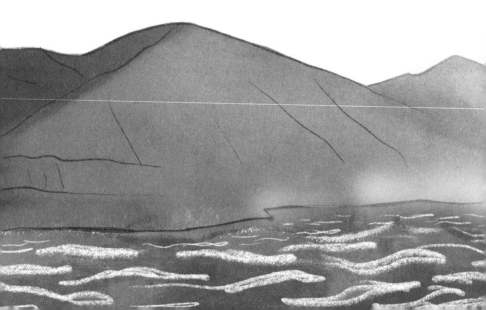

brand-new! The wooden helm gleamed, and the seagull that had perched there was gone. *He'll be back,* Sofia knew.

As the wheel spun to the left, her eyes flitted toward the coast. Cliffs rose through the mist toward the gray sky above. "Look at those rocks!" she cried.

Max followed her gaze. The charcoal rocks looked like tall, skinny blocks perched on a dark sea. "Is that black water?" he asked.

Sofia pushed her bangs aside. "Black sand, I think," she said. "I saw some when my family went to Saint Lucia in the Caribbean. The sand was made of the lava from volcanoes." She shivered. "But this place is too cold to be a Caribbean island! Where are we?"

Max pointed toward the trapdoor that led belowdecks. "I know how to find out," he said with a grin.

"The atlas!" said Sofia. "Of course!" In their past adventures, the magical atlas in *Wind Rider*'s cabin had always shown them exactly where they were.

Together, they raced belowdecks. Sofia slid down the metal ladder and darted past the tidy galley kitchen. Past the polished dining table and chairs and the round portholes above. She skidded to a stop in front of a thick atlas resting on a table.

As the pages of the book fluttered, Sofia held her breath. The book fell open to the map of a large island. "Iceland!" she shouted—so loud that Max jumped.

"I'm right behind you!" he said, laughing. But his own heart raced as he peered at the page. "Wow, maybe we'll see the northern lights. Grandpa's brother went fishing in Iceland once, and he said he saw the whole sky light up!"

"Or maybe we'll swim in a hot spring," said Sofia. "The water comes out of the ground hot. I read that people in Iceland sometimes use it to heat their houses!"

"Wait," said Max. "We could see if *Wind Rider* has given us any clues about what we're doing here." He pointed at the elegantly carved sea chest in the corner.

"Right," said Sofia. "Let's take a look!" The magical old chest always held the gear they would need for their adventure.

The lid creaked as Max peered inside. "Brrr. Looks like we're heading into the cold," he said, pulling out a couple of parkas. "And into the water!" He reached for two sets of waders—long rubber pants with attached boots and shoulder straps. Max had worn them before when Grandpa had taken him river fishing.

"What's in these?" asked Sofia, lifting two blue backpacks out of the chest.

She unzipped one and pulled out several rolled-up towels. "Uh-oh. We really *are* going to get wet!"

Max dug past the towels in the second backpack and found a shovel and gloves. "Looks like we'll be doing some digging, too. But this is an awfully short shovel." He bent low over the shovel, which was only about a foot long. "Wait, I think it's growing!" He slid the handle slowly upward, wobbling his arms as if the shovel had come to life.

Sofia laughed out loud. "Extendable shovels—cool! What else is in here?" She dug in the pockets of her backpack. "Green recycling bags and"—she dug deeper— "beaded necklaces. Wait, we've seen these before. They help us communicate in other languages, remember?"

"Mm-hmm." Max was already tugging on his waders and parka. He stuck his shoes into his backpack and slung it over his shoulder. "All right, I'm ready."

"Ready for what?" asked Sofia.

"I don't know. Hiking? Fishing?" He clomped back to the ladder in his waders. "C'mon, let's go!"

Sofia pulled on her gear and followed him up. When they reached the deck, they saw that they were getting closer to the black sand beach.

As Sofia studied the coast, a flash of white streaked through the waves below. Then another. She raced along the deck to take a closer look. "It's a pod of whales," she called. "White whales!"

Max saw them, too. When one swiveled its head toward him, he gasped. "It looks like a dolphin, but bigger!" As if in response, the whales chirped and squealed. One whistled before slapping its tail against the water.

Sofia laughed out loud, barely believing what she was seeing. "They're so chatty!"

Max grinned. "They sure are. I've never seen—or heard—whales like that back home."

As *Wind Rider* drifted closer to shore, the whales began to round the rocky coast. Sofia gazed longingly after them until the last whale disappeared. "What do you think they were saying to us?" she asked— just as *Wind Rider* dropped its anchor and slowed to a stop.

Max glanced at the shoreline, which was still a short distance away. He smiled. "I think they were saying it's time to make like a whale and get wet."

CHAPTER 3
PUFFIN PATROL

Sofia stared at the waves below, wondering how deep the water might be. Then she heard voices. She glanced up and saw a boy and a girl crossing the black sand beach.

"Let's catch up to them," said Max. "We're wearing waders for a reason!" He grabbed his backpack and climbed carefully down the ladder attached to *Wind Rider*'s hull. He stepped into the water, lowering his foot slowly until he felt the sandy seabed below. The sea was only knee-high, but it was freezing! Max shivered, but his waders kept him dry.

Sofia followed him down. "We'll have to hurry if we're going to catch them!" she said. But wading through the icy waves felt like running in slow motion.

When she finally reached the slick black sand, she glanced at the tower of rocks rising through the mist. Birds called to one another as they circled high above. Then someone called to *her*—the boy on the beach. But she couldn't understand a word he was saying. "Hæ, þurfið þið hjálp?"

I need my necklace! Sofia realized. She pulled the beads from her backpack and slipped them on. As Max stepped out of the waves, she motioned to him to do the same.

"Hi," the boy onshore said. "Do you need help?" He waved with one hand and straightened his knit cap with the other.

"Hello!" said Sofia. "We're fine, thanks."

The red-haired boy stepped closer. "I'm Gunnar Magnusson." He gestured toward the blond girl at his side. "This is my twin sister, Agnes Magnusdóttir."

Agnes smiled shyly from beneath the fur-lined hood of her purple parka.

"Wait," said Max. "If you're twins, why do you have different last names?"

Gunnar laughed. "You're new to Iceland, aren't you? I couldn't tell at first,

because you speak Icelandic quite well. Here, your last name tells who your father is. Our father is Magnus, so I am the son of Magnus and Agnes is the 'dóttir' of Magnus."

Sofia cocked her head. "I get it! So I would be Sofia Tomásdóttir, the daughter of my dad, Tomás."

Agnes nodded. "Welcome, Sofia," she said warmly. She didn't seem as chatty as her brother, but her eyes twinkled.

"What brings you to Iceland?" asked Gunnar.

"We're here to, um, see the wildlife," Max said quickly. *It's true*, he reminded himself. *We just don't know which animals we're here to help yet!*

"We already saw a pod of whales!" said Sofia. "White ones."

"Ah, beluga whales," said Gunnar. "We also have humpbacks."

Max grinned. "We have humpback whales back home!" Suddenly, Iceland didn't feel quite so far away from Starry Bay.

"If you like wildlife, it's good we met," said Gunnar. "We're part of the local Puffin Patrol. We're on our way to a puffin colony right now." He pointed toward the rocky cliffs, where seabirds swooped in and out of the rocks. "Would you like to come?"

Sofia's heart leaped. She had seen puffins only once before, during another adventure on *Wind Rider* to Scotland.

"We'd love to," she said.

"Definitely!" said Max. *Is this why we're here?* he wondered. *Did* Wind Rider *bring us here to help the puffins?* He quickly took off his waders and changed back into his shoes.

As Sofia fell into step beside Agnes, the sun peeked through the clouds, casting a sheen across the black sand. Sofia dodged a clump of seaweed just as Agnes nudged her shoulder.

"Speaking of puffins . . . ," she said.

"Where?" Sofia followed Agnes's gaze toward the cliffs. Then she saw it—a squat

puffin perched beside a bush. It had wide orange feet, black feathers, and a bright white belly, as though it was wearing a tuxedo. Its beak was striped and brightly colored. Seconds later, it waddled off the rocks and took flight.

"Its wings are beating so fast!" said Max. "It looks like a black-and-white football."

Gunnar chuckled. Then he picked up his pace in the sand, waving for the others to follow.

"So what is the Puffin Patrol?" asked Sofia, skipping to catch up.

"Kids like us who look out for the puffins," said Gunnar. "The patrol started because pufflings were getting lost. When baby puffins leave their nest, they're supposed to follow the moonlight out to sea. But sometimes they get confused by the lights on shore. They head toward town, and we have to set them back on the right path."

Sofia shot Max a glance. *We did that with baby turtles!* she remembered. He raised his eyebrows, as if remembering the same thing. On their first adventure, *Wind Rider* had taken them to a beach where baby sea turtles were hatching, and they led the turtles to the sea using a light-house's lamp. *Can we help the pufflings the same way?* Sofia wondered. She looked around but didn't see any lighthouses.

She glanced back at her footprints in the jet-black sand. They led away from *Wind Rider* . . . but toward adventure. Encouraged, she quickened her pace.

CHAPTER 4
THE CLIFF'S EDGE

"This way," said Gunnar. They rounded the base of the cliffs, heading toward a steep dirt path. "Nowhere to go but up!"

Max let out a low whistle as he craned his head to look at the top of the cliff. His backpack suddenly felt very heavy. "I think I'll wait for the cable car," he joked.

"C'mon," said Sofia, nudging him. "Remember, there are puffins at the top!" She started up the path so quickly, she nearly passed Gunnar.

Max followed, but he soon felt sweat sliding down his neck from the effort. He unzipped his parka, hoping the breeze would cool him down. "Do you hike this path a lot?" he asked Gunnar, who wasn't the slightest bit out of breath.

Gunnar nodded. "Our friends take turns with us. We check on the puffins and report back." He patted the walkie-talkie at his side. "Everyone in the Puffin Patrol gets one of these."

"And a badge?" asked Sofia, pointing at the round patch sewn to Agnes's jacket. A cute puffin was embroidered against a blue sky.

"Yes," said Agnes. "And notebooks for jotting down what we see. It's all very official."

Sofia sighed. "I'd love to be part of the Puffin Patrol—and to hike this pretty path every day." The steep, rocky trail had gradually become a grassy slope blanketed with wild flowers.

As they neared the top of the trail, Agnes stopped. "The fjord is the most beautiful part," she said. "Look! It's the valley over there that runs out to sea." To their right, the mountains gave way to a U-shaped valley. A thin waterfall trickled down the cliffs toward the sea, the water sparkling in the distance.

Sofia stepped toward the edge to get a better view, but a stiff gust of wind pushed her backward.

"Careful!" Gunnar called. "Puffins dig their burrows out of the cliffside just below your feet."

Sofia froze. Was the ground beneath her moving, or was she imagining it? She slowly stepped back toward the trail.

"It's all right," said Agnes. "Come look at the other burrows!" She led Sofia to a small rocky ridge and knelt behind it.

"Puffin burrows?" Max hurried toward the ridge. He crouched beside

Sofia and gazed over the rocks.

Grassy mounds stretched out before them. Here and there, Max could see deep round holes in the earth, masked by tufts of grass.

When a puffin poked its colorful bill out of a hole, Sofia gasped. "I see one!" she whispered. The puffin crept from the hole and waddled forward on bright orange feet.

Soon another puffin popped out of a burrow. And then another. As they perched on the grass, like little soldiers standing guard, Agnes and Gunnar began jotting notes in their Puffin Patrol notebooks.

"Where are the chicks?" whispered Max.

"Deep in the burrows," said Gunnar. "It's not fledgling season yet—the pufflings can't fly. So they stay in the burrows, where they're safest from foxes and hawks. But you might see one peeking out."

Max scanned the closest burrows. When a tuft of grass quivered, he held his breath. Then he saw it—the fluffy gray head and tiny gray beak of a puffling. "There!" he whispered.

The puffling cheeped weakly, and Sofia bit her lip. "It doesn't look very strong. Where are its parents?" She studied the grass nearby, where plastic bags, bottles, and other garbage was scattered everywhere. "And why is there so much trash here? I can't believe people would litter near puffin burrows!"

Agnes sighed. "It's actually the puffins who bring the plastic here, because they think it's food. See?" She pointed.

A puffin was flying in for a wobbly landing. In its beak, it held a scrap of plastic.

Sofia's heart sank. "No wonder the puffling looks so weak!" she whispered. "But why do puffins mistake plastic for food?" The plastic sure didn't look like a fish.

"I don't know," said Gunnar. "But we've seen other puffins trying to feed it to their babies."

When the puffin dropped the piece of plastic, a gust of wind swept it across the grass. Sofia leaped up to get it—before the puffin could attempt feeding it to its chick!

The plastic skittered across the rocky ground and came to rest a couple of yards away from the cliff's edge. As Sofia bent to pick it up, she saw something large and white stretched across the black sand below. What was it?

The creature thumped its tail, and Sofia's heart froze. She sucked in her breath. *A whale*, she realized. *A beluga whale!*

Max was already by her side. "Whoa," he said.

"That whale is beached," said Sofia, her eyes wide. "It's stuck on the sand. We've got to help it!"

CHAPTER 5
SAVE THE WHALE!

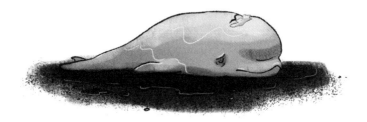

"We've got to get down there right now!" said Max, as Gunnar and Agnes came to peer over the cliff edge. He started for the trail.

"Not that way! It'll take too long and we might not have enough time," said Gunnar. "Follow me. There's a shortcut."

"Maybe *this* is why *Wind Rider* brought us here," Sofia muttered to Max. "To save the whale. C'mon!"

Max tightened the straps on his backpack and hurried after her.

Gunnar led them to a steep, rocky path that hugged a trickling waterfall. As Max picked his way across the moss-covered rocks, the wind whipped wildly. He hung on to every shrub and tree he could find.

"Take your time," called Agnes from behind. "The rocks can be slippery."

When the path finally leveled out,

Gunnar stopped. "Watch your step," he said. Then he leaped across a narrow gorge. Sofia followed, bounding as if she had springs for legs.

"You want me to do *what* now?" said Max as he approached the gorge. The gap between the rocks was only a few feet wide, but he couldn't see the bottom. If he slipped, how far would he fall?

"It's all right," said Agnes. "I'll show you how." She leaped across the gap with ease.

Max swallowed hard and glanced at Sofia, who waited for him on the other side. "You've got this," she said, holding out her hand. "Do it for the whale!"

With that thought, Max blew out his breath. Then he took a few steps backward and raced toward the gorge. He jumped . . .

and flew so far over it, he missed Sofia's out-stretched hand and landed in a heap. "Oops."

Sofia helped him up. "I knew you could do it," she said with a grin. "Let's go!"

Farther down the trail, Gunnar reached for his walkie-talkie. "I'll call the other Puffin Patrollers," he said over his shoulder. "And the aquatic vet. We're going to need all the help we can get!"

"Will they get here in time?" Sofia asked Agnes.

Agnes studied the water below. "I hope so," she said. "Look, the poor beluga's family is waiting."

Sofia glanced toward the sea, where ten or twelve pale whales skimmed the surface of the water. They circled slowly, as if watching—and waiting. Her heart swelled. "Oh, we have to hurry!" she cried, breaking into a sprint.

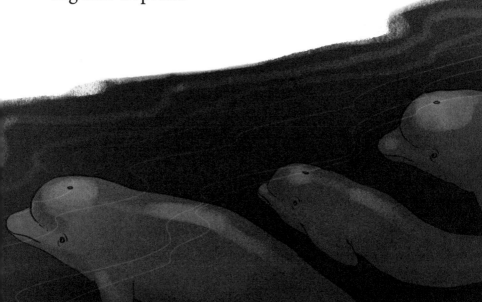

But when they finally reached the beach, Gunnar held up his hand. "Try not to scare the whale," he said.

They tiptoed across the black sand. Max marveled at the creature stretched out before them. The creamy white whale lay

on its belly. It was almost as long as a small car. Its sides were heaving, as if it were struggling to breathe.

As they stepped closer, the whale eyed them warily and thumped its head up and down, as if trying to swim away.

Then Max saw a crinkly mass pressed across the whale's round head. "That looks like a plastic bag," he cried.

Sofia gasped. "The bag is covering the whale's blowhole. If it can't breathe, it'll suffocate!" she said.

"Maybe that's why it beached," said Agnes.

"What do we do?" Sofia asked. She turned toward Gunnar, who lowered his walkie-talkie. "The Puffin Patrol says the vet is out on another call," he said, worry creasing his forehead. "It will take time for her to get here."

We don't have time! thought Sofia. She set her jaw. "I'll do it. I'll get the bag." The words flew out of her mouth before she could think them through.

"Are you sure?" asked Max.

Sofia nodded and licked her lips. She stepped slowly toward the whale, who watched her with cautious eyes. It bobbed its head again and squealed, the bag tightening over its blowhole.

Can I do it? Sofia wondered, her chest tight. *Will the whale trust me enough to let me help?*

CHAPTER 6
THE SMILING FISH

Sofia took another step toward the beached whale. She had never stood beside such a large animal. But she knew what she had to do.

"It's okay, whale. I'm going to help you," she whispered. As she reached out a hand to stroke the whale's smooth, slippery skin, it let out a high-pitched squeal.

"I'm sorry," Sofia whispered, pulling her hand away. "I won't hurt you."

She reached slowly for the bag, careful not to spook the whale again. She stood on tiptoe, the sand sinking beneath her feet. Could she get the bag without leaning on the frightened whale?

"Take my hand!" she said to Max. He gripped one of her hands as she reached for the plastic bag with the other. She wobbled once, twice . . . then clutched the plastic bag with her fingertips. "Got it!"

Relief flooded through her chest. The whale seemed to calm down, too. Its sides rose gently as it took a long, deep breath.

"Nice work!" said Agnes, her cheeks flushed.

But as Sofia glanced down at the bag in her hands, she gasped. "Bay Fish Grill?

That's the restaurant in Starry Bay!"

"No way. Let me see." Max stared at the Bay Fish Grill logo, and the smiling fish stared back. "Yep, I'd know that face anywhere," he said with a groan. "Bay Fish Grill is a chain of restaurants, so this might not be from Starry Bay. But it definitely traveled across the ocean to get here."

Agnes sighed. "Iceland banned plastic bags like this," she said. "But we can't control what gets into the sea from other countries."

"I'm sorry," said Sofia, gazing back at the whale. "Sorry to you, and sorry to the puffins who are feeding plastic to their babies." Then she began to pace, leaving a trail of footprints in the sand. "We have to get this whale back out to sea. But it's too heavy to push or pull. What do we do?"

"Keep it wet!" Gunnar said, tucking his walkie-talkie into his pocket. "My friends say the vet wants us to keep the whale wet so that it stays cool and its skin doesn't dry out. Then we need to dig a channel beside it. When the tide comes in, the channel will fill with water and the whale can swim back out to sea."

Agnes sighed. "How will we keep the whale wet? We don't have hoses or anything to carry water in!"

"Wait!" said Sofia, sliding the backpack off her shoulder. "Will these work?" She tugged the towels out of the pack.

"Yes!" said Agnes, brightening at once. "Hand me one." Together, they rushed toward the surf to wet the towels.

As Sofia carefully placed the first wet towel on the whale's back, she held her breath—waiting for the whale to squeal again or pull away. Instead, it chirped softly and relaxed its head onto the sand.

"That feels good, doesn't it?" Sofia whispered.

Max zipped open his own backpack, and soon all four kids were laying cool wet towels across the whale's back, steering clear of its blowhole.

"Time to dig the trench?" said Max. "If only we had shovels . . ." He shot Sofia a grin and then reached for his backpack.

"Oh, wait! We *do* have shovels!"

"Wow!" said Agnes, laughing. "You two are very prepared."

It's easy to be prepared when you've got a magical sailboat, thought Max, as he dug at the sand beside the whale. *It knew just what we needed.*

Sofia began to dig, too, while Gunnar and Agnes made sure the towels on the whale's back stayed wet. The damp black sand was heavy, though, and hard to lift with the shovel. When Sofia stopped for a break, Agnes held out her hand. "My turn," she offered.

"Thanks!" said Sofia, handing over the shovel. As she stepped away from the whale, it watched her with wise dark eyes. "You know we're trying to help you, don't you?" said Sofia soothingly. "You seem awfully smart."

"Beluga whales are very smart," said Gunnar as he reached for Max's shovel. "Just like dolphins. They're in the same family."

Sofia nodded. "I've read that they're really social, too."

"And chatty," Max reminded her. "Remember how they were squawking, chirping, and whistling when we first saw them out at sea? They were communicating with each other—and maybe with us, too!"

Sofia smiled, remembering. Then she glanced over her shoulder at the waves, where she hoped the pod of whales was still waiting.

"When the tide comes in, you'll be free," she said, turning back toward the whale. "You can go join your family."

But as the waves lapped against the shore, the whale thumped its head against the sand.

Sofia's stomach twisted. *Will the tide come soon enough?*

Chapter 7
RACE AGAINST THE TIDE

Max heard the buzz of a motorboat and studied the waves. "Are those your friends?" he asked Gunnar.

"Yes," said Gunnar. "At last!"

The small blue boat was just rounding the rocky bend into the inlet. Max heard gasps and saw the kids in the boat pointing into the waves.

"Belugas!" The cry drifted across the water to the shore.

"The pod must still be out there," said Max.

Sofia strained her eyes to see who was in the boat. "Did your friends bring the vet?" she asked.

Agnes shook her head. "It doesn't look like it. The vet must be busy with another emergency. But our friends will help us with the whale until she gets here."

When the boat slid ashore, three kids spilled out, carrying buckets and towels. Gunnar introduced them. "This is Benny," he said, pointing toward a boy in a black jacket. "And Lana." A girl with a long side braid dipped her head. "And Gefn." Gefn zipped up her pink puffer jacket and grinned. "This is Max and Sofia," Gunnar told them. "They love animals as much as we do!" Lana waved her phone in the air as she crossed the beach. "We have the aquatic vet on speakerphone. She'll talk us through what to do until she gets here."

"Hello, kids!" A friendly woman's voice

rose from the phone above the sound of the surf. "I'm going to have you do a quick exam, okay? First check the whale for any injuries to its tail, fins, or skin. Look for gashes or bites."

Max followed Benny toward the whale's head. The boy pointed toward a dark scar just above the blowhole. "Is that an injury?" asked Max.

"An old one, I think," said Benny. "It looks like it healed."

As friendly Gefn followed Sofia from fin to fin, the whale swiveled its head to watch them. "Do you see anything?" Gefn asked.

Sofia blew out her breath. "No, thank goodness."

"Are the whale's eyes open and bright?" the vet asked.

"Yes!" said Sofia. "It's been watching us." She gazed back into the whale's wise eyes and smiled.

"Good, good. And how long is it?" asked the vet.

Max, Gunnar, and Benny paced alongside the whale, trying to guess its length. Gunnar and Benny walked toe-to-heel, but since Max knew his shoe was shorter than a foot, he took slightly larger steps. Max

counted off ten footsteps out loud.

"So about ten feet," said the vet. "And it sounds like it's healthy. I think that plastic bag over the blowhole must be what caused the whale to beach. Have you finished digging the trench?"

Benny rounded the whale's tail. "I think it should be deeper," he said. "Hand me a shovel."

"I'll help, too," said Lana, setting down her phone on an overturned bucket.

Sofia watched them dig, wishing there were more than two shovels. Then she heard Gunnar shout. "Tide's coming in!"

"Quick, everybody dig!" cried Max.

He dropped to his knees and began scooping up sand with his hands. Sofia and the others joined him, digging furiously as the foamy surf crept farther up the beach.

When the waves reached the trench and began to fill it with water, the whale thumped its tail, as if it were excited, too.

"Keep digging!" cried Benny as he pitched a shovelful of sand over his shoulder.

Sofia was digging so fast, she could barely catch her breath. Her hands were freezing numb, but she ignored the cold. "Make it wider!" she cried. "So there's enough water for the whale to swim free!"

Beside her, Gefn scrabbled at the sand, too—like a dog digging up a bone.

When the trench was full of water, Sofia sat back on her heels. "Now what?" she said, her heart pounding in her ears.

"Now the whale needs a little help," said the vet on speakerphone. "Roll it into the channel. Get on one side of the whale and gently push."

Max locked eyes with Sofia. This wasn't the biggest whale he'd ever seen, but it looked heavy. Would they be strong enough? *We'll have to be*, he decided.

As they all lined up alongside the whale, Max took a deep breath. "On the count of three!" he cried. "One, two . . ." He set his hands on the whale's smooth, wet skin. "*Three!*"

Chapter 8
THE PLASTIC PROBLEM

All seven kids pushed together, leaning against the whale's rubbery skin.

I hope we don't hurt it! thought Sofia. The whale rocked sideways, but then slowly rolled back.

"Again!" hollered Max. "One, two . . . three!"

This time, Sofia pushed as hard as she could. Her feet slipped in the sand, but she dug her heels in and pushed harder.

Finally, the whale rolled and splashed into the water-filled channel.

"Yes!" cried Max. He pumped his fist and held his hand up for a high five.

But Sofia wasn't quite ready to celebrate. "The channel looks so narrow," she said. "Is there room for the whale to swim?"

"Give it a moment," said the vet in a reassuring voice.

Sofia held her breath. *Go!* she wanted to cry. *Swim!*

The whale shifted slightly in the channel. It rolled once and lifted its head above the waves. Then, with a chirp and a flip of its tail, it darted toward the rolling surf.

"We did it!" whooped Max. He slapped Gunnar's palm, and Sofia threw her arms around Agnes and Lana.

"Well done!" said the vet. "It sounds like you saved the beluga."

Sofia sighed. "I wish we could save *every* beached whale. And every hungry puffling." She suddenly remembered something that had been nagging at her. "That plastic bag isn't the only litter we saw today. We saw a puffin trying to feed a piece of plastic to its chick! Why would it mistake plastic for food?"

The vet sighed. "Puffins hunt using their sense of smell," she explained. "Plastic that's been floating in seawater can smell like fish, so puffins think they're bringing fish back to their babies."

"That's so sad," said Sofia. "I wish we could do something about it."

"You've certainly done your part today," the vet reassured her.

But as the kids said goodbye to the vet and hung up the phone, Gefn cocked her head. "This plastic problem—maybe we should have a Puffin Patrol meeting about it at the ice cream parlor."

Max's stomach grumbled. "Did someone say ice cream?" he said, wringing out a towel. "Sign me up!"

"Good!" said Lana. "It'll be our treat, and

we can fit seven people in the boat. C'mon!"

As they all climbed into the motorboat, Sofia let the Puffin Patrol members take the chairs, and she and Max shared the padded seat at the back. Benny started the engine and steered them out of the fjord.

As the boat hummed along through the waves, Sofia craned her neck, searching the cliffs for signs of puffins. But a mist rolled in, and she lost sight of the cliffs altogether.

"Almost there," said Benny. They hugged the coast, the black sand giving way to a green valley dotted with colorful houses.

He set a course for a pier and then drifted up alongside it and cut the motor.

"This way!" said Gefn. "Ice cream, here we come!"

Sofia followed her up the pier and toward the cluster of houses. Each one seemed to be a different shade of bright: royal blue, sunny yellow, leafy green, and candy red. "Even the roof is red!" said Sofia.

As the sun disappeared behind a cloud, Max shivered. "Are you sure the ice cream shop will be open?" he said. "Or will it have turned into a hot chocolate shop?"

Gunnar laughed. "Don't worry," he said.

"We eat ice cream all year round."

When they reached the shop, he led them through the door. Tubs of ice cream beckoned from behind a glass counter. Max read the labels one by one: "Chocolate, strawberry, banana, licorice . . . wait, licorice?"

"My favorite!" said Gunnar.

Sofia bounced on her toes. "My favorite is chocolate." When it was her turn to order, she asked for a large scoop of chocolate dipped in a chocolate shell and topped with chocolate sprinkles.

As she slid into a booth with her cone,

Gunnar called the Puffin Patrol meeting to order. "All right, gang," he said, "we've got work to do!"

"And puffins to save," said Max. But as he bit into his cone, the caramel shell cracked and toppings spilled across the table. "Oops," he said, scooping them up. "First, I've got to save my ice cream."

Sofia giggled and handed him a napkin.

"So what can we do about the plastic

pollution?" asked Agnes. She opened her notebook.

Sofia sighed. "Well, you said Iceland cut down on its plastic. But it still floats here from other countries and ends up in the water and on beaches."

Max wiped his chin. "Maybe we could clean up the beach," he said.

Sofia's eyes widened. "Yes," she said. "Good idea!"

"And all we'll need is some recycling bags," said Gefn.

Max patted his backpack. "We've got some in our trusty backpacks," he said.

"They're biodegradable," Sofia added, remembering the word she'd seen printed on the lime-green bags. "Hey, maybe we can clean up the area around the puffin burrows, too!"

"Yes!" said Agnes. "We should do that first, to protect the pufflings."

Sofia could hardly wait to get started. But as she finished her ice cream and slid out of the booth, Agnes reached for her hand.

"Wait," said Agnes. "There's one more order of business. I think we should make Sofia and Max honorary members of the Puffin Patrol. All in favor?"

Six hands shot up. Then Sofia realized she was raising her own. "Oops!" she said, lowering it.

When Agnes pinned a blue puffin badge to her parka, Sofia felt as if her whole body were floating sky-high.

She could tell Max was excited, too, because for once, he had actually beaten her out the door.

CHAPTER 9
THE HUNGRY PUFFLING

As Sofia crouched behind the rocky ridge, she studied the sky, watching for puffins.

The Puffin Patrol had spent the afternoon cleaning up the burrows. While most of the puffins were away fishing for food, the patrol had carefully picked up trash from the grassy mounds. *No matter what happens, we tried to help the pufflings*, Sofia reminded herself. *We did what we could!*

"What time is it?" she asked Max for the third time.

"Time for dinner—finally," he said. He pointed at the puffin landing on the burrows. As it waddled forward, a floppy fish swung from its beak. "Mmm, delicious," said Max. "No more plastic fish!"

Sofia crossed her fingers, hoping she might recognize the puffling they'd seen earlier. As more birds returned from the sea, she waited. Then a flutter of wings caught her by surprise. A puffin landed a few feet away and dropped two juicy fish in front of a burrow.

"Those are herring!" whispered Agnes. "What a tasty meal for the puffling."

"But where is it?" asked Sofia, straining to see. When she heard a *cheep*, she held her breath.

As the puffling popped out of the hole, Sofia grinned. Just like the others, the fuzzy-headed chick had a dark gray beak and feet, with none of its mother's bright colors. But it was *so* cute! It cheeped again and then began to gobble up its dinner.

"Yes!" whispered Sofia. "We saved the

beached whale *and* cleaned up the puffin burrows." *We did what we came here to do,* she realized, her heart swelling with joy and pride.

As more puffins landed among the burrows, Max spotted one bird that *wasn't* a puffin. He nudged Sofia. "Look!"

The seagull landed on a rock and stared at them, bobbing its sleek white head.

"Our gull!" whispered Sofia.

Max nodded. "It must be time to go."

"You're right," said Agnes with a sigh. She stood up. "It's getting late."

"But we did well!" said Gunnar, hoisting a full recycling bag. "Now we just have to *keep* the burrows clean."

"And the beaches, too," said Gefn. She linked arms with Sofia. "Can you and Max help us clean the beach tomorrow?"

Sofia sighed. "I wish we could! But I think we're leaving tonight." As she glanced at the gull, it seemed to agree. It flapped its wings and flew over the edge of the cliff, toward the water below.

Agnes patted the badge on Sofia's sleeve. "Well, you'll always be members of our Puffin Patrol." She gave Sofia a sweet smile.

On the hike back to the beach, Max kept one eye on the rocky trail and one eye on the sea. *Is our beluga out there?* he wondered. *Will the whales and puffins be safer now that the Puffin Patrol is working on the plastic problem?* He hoped so.

A short while later, he and Sofia were hugging their new friends and wading back out to *Wind Rider*. As they stood on the deck, waving goodbye to the Puffin Patrol, Sofia glanced at her badge. *You'll always be members of our Puffin Patrol,* Agnes had said. The memory made Sofia smile.

Max heard the creak of the anchor

lifting. The sails unfurled, and *Wind Rider* moved slowly away from shore. Then he spotted something in the waves below. "Whales!"

Sofia joined him at the bow just as a beluga lifted its head. It whistled and sent a spray of water sky-high. Sofia laughed as she wiped the mist from her face. "That whale is swimming so close!" she said.

When Max saw the dark scar above the whale's blowhole, his heart leaped. "It's our whale," he said. "The one we saved!"

As the whale surfaced again, Sofia studied its friendly face. It let out an excited

squeal, and Sofia did, too. "It *is* our whale!"

The other whales let out a chorus of chirps and squeaks. One rolled in the water, showing off its belly. Another slapped its tail against the waves. "Maybe they came to say thank you," said Sofia.

"Maybe," said Max. "Or to say goodbye." When a brisk wind nudged him off-balance, he reached for the rail, ready for the journey back to Starry Bay. And as the helm began to spin, he squeezed his eyes shut. He felt Sofia beside him, bracing against the gusty wind.

At last, the deck stopped rocking. Max felt a gentle thud and opened his eyes to the mangrove forest. Branches rustled overhead, and the gull took flight.

Max sighed. "I miss Iceland already."

"At least we have souvenirs!" said Sofia. "So we'll never forget our friends there." She unpinned the Puffin Patrol badge from her sleeve. "Let's leave our badges here—belowdecks, where they'll be safe." She crossed the splintered deck of *Wind Rider*, which was once again weathered and worn.

Max followed her down the rusty ladder into the dark cabin and handed her his badge.

Sofia tucked both badges on a shelf beside souvenirs from past *Wind Rider* adventures: a turtle eggshell, macaw feathers, and seals carved from wood.

Until next time, she thought, gazing at the treasures. Then she headed back toward the ladder.

Max and Sofia left *Wind Rider* nestled among the mangrove trees. But as they started along the path toward the beach, Sofia squatted to pick up a straw. "More plastic," she said. "It's everywhere!"

"Where's the Puffin Patrol when you need them?" said Max. Then a thought struck. "Hey, could we start a beach patrol of our own?"

Sofia's eyes lit up. "Yes!" she said. "All we need are some recycling bags."

"Grandpa keeps some on his fishing boat," said Max. "Meet you on the beach?"

Sofia grinned and set off past the ice cream shop. Max veered right and jogged down the wobbly boards of the dock. Waves lapped along either side, and the smell of seawater greeted him. When he reached Grandpa's fishing boat, he quickly found the bags on the deck near some rope and other supplies.

By the time Max got to the beach, Sofia had already found a plastic fork and a Styrofoam cup.

"What are you doing?" asked a girl with a sunburned nose and large glasses.

Max puffed out his chest. "We're the newly formed Starry Bay Beach Patrol," he said. "Doing very official business." He leaned over and dramatically dug a drinking straw from the sand.

The girl watched for a moment and then asked, "Can my brother and I help?"

"Sure!" said Max. "You can be our newest members." He shot Sofia a grin, remembering how Gunnar and Agnes had invited them into their own club.

"We need all the help we can get!" agreed Sofia. "I don't know how we'll ever keep this whole beach clean."

Then she remembered how they had helped the beluga and the pufflings. *That's how we'll do it*, she thought with a smile. *One piece of plastic at a time.*

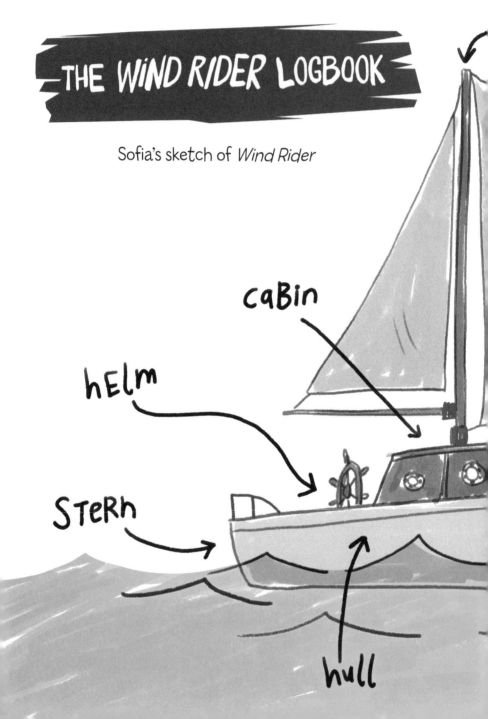

mast

SeaGull

Sail

porThole

bow

winDRiDER

aNchoR

OUR ICELANDIC ADVENTURE

We never know where *Wind Rider* will take us next! This time we visited Iceland, which lies in the cold waters of the North Atlantic Ocean. It's a rocky island nation with lava fields, volcanoes, and hot springs (pools of water that are naturally heated by underground volcanic activity). Plenty of animals live there, from Atlantic puffins nesting on high cliffs to fluffy arctic foxes that hunt inland to beluga whales, which travel in groups called pods in the surrounding seas. Iceland has banned single-use plastics to help fight pollution and keep its beaches clean.

GREENLAND SEA

Greenland

Iceland

Faroe Islands

NORTH ATLANTIC
OCEAN

United
Kingdom

Ireland

N

SOFIA'S ANIMAL FACTS

We loved seeing Atlantic puffins, with their amazing colorful beaks and big orange feet . . . and we got up close to a beluga whale, too! Here are my top facts about puffins and beluga whales.

- Atlantic puffins are sometimes called the penguins of the north, sea parrots, or even clowns of the sea.

- Those beautiful beaks actually change color throughout the year. They are dull gray in winter, then turn bright orange and yellow in spring!

- Beluga whales are among the smallest types of whale. They have bumpy foreheads and are sometimes called white whales because of their color.

■ Beluga whales are great communicators. They make chirps, clicks, and whistles to talk to each other, and they can also mimic sounds!

■ While puffins and beluga whales are not endangered right now, they do face some threats, such as pollution of the seas with plastic and oil spills, sound pollution, which makes it difficult for belugas to communicate, and overfishing, which is when people take so much fish from the sea that there's not enough left for animals to feed on.

HOW CAN WE HELP CLEAN THE BEACH?

We decided to organize a beach cleanup in Starry Bay. If you're near a beach, why not do the same? Here are some tips to get you started.

Ask an adult to help. In some areas, you might need to get permission. Or you could join a beach cleanup that's already been organized.

Early fall is a good time to go, after the summer crowds that leave trash behind.

It's a team effort! Invite your friends and family. You could even put up posters to let everyone in the community know what you're doing.

Bring recycling bags (biodegradable are best!) and gloves. And don't forget sunscreen—or hats and coats, depending on the weather!

Have fun and feel proud! You're doing your bit to keep the beach clean and to help the local wildlife.